Tell Me About Heaven

Welcome Home

Story by
Randy Alcorn

Paintings by
Ron DiCianni

CROSSWAY BOOKS

A PUBLISHING MINISTRY OF GOOD NEWS PUBLISHERS ∞ WHEATON, ILLINOIS

Tell Me About Heaven
Text copyright © 2007 by Randy Alcorn
Illustrations copyright © 2007 by Ron DiCianni
Published by Crossway Books
        a publishing ministry of Good News Publishers
        1300 Crescent Street
        Wheaton, Illinois 60187

Illustrations: Ron DiCianni

Cover design: Josh Dennis
Interior design: Josh Dennis
First printing 2007
Printed in the United States of America

Ron DiCianni is represented by and this work was produced with assistance from: Tapestry Productions, Inc, 43980 Mahlon Vail Circle, Suite 803, Temecula, CA 92592. To see more of Ron DiCianni's paintings please visit: www.TapestryProductions.com.

LIBRARY OF CONGRESS CATALOGING-IN-PUBLICATION DATA
Alcorn, Randy C.
Tell me about heaven / Randy Alcorn ; [illustrations by] Ron DiCianni.
    p. cm.
ISBN-13: 978-1-58134-853-8 (hc : alk. paper)
ISBN-10: 1-58134-853-3 (hc : alk. paper)
1. Heaven--Christianity--Juvenile literature. I. DiCianni, Ron. II. Title.
BT846.3.A435 2007
236'.24--dc22   2007005145

LB		15	14	13	12	11	10	09	08	07
15	14	13	12	11	10	9	8	7	6	5	4	3	2	1

To my beloved grandchildren:

Jake Stump, Matthew Franklin, Tyler Stump and Jack Franklin.

May you live for Jesus, with the New Earth in view.

For Nicky, my first grandson. The doctors gave me little hope of ever seeing you,

but God granted my wish! We're going to have a blast in Heaven...

Contents

For to me, to live is Christ and to die is gain....

I desire to depart and be with Christ, which is better by far.

PHILIPPIANS 1:21, 23

CHAPTER ONE

Into His Arms

Every June since he was three, Jake had spent two weeks with Papa and Grammy. They lived in Oregon, out in the country. Trees and streams were everywhere. Jake loved fishing in the lake and looking at the dark night sky through Papa's telescope. He loved smelling Grammy's roses blooming and eating the best strawberries he'd ever tasted.

But that cloudy Monday afternoon, as his dad turned up the road to Papa and Grammy's, Jake didn't feel his usual excitement.

Papa and Grammy had stayed at Jake's house for a week at Christmas, and Grammy didn't feel well. Then one cold night in February, she had a heart attack.

The doctors did their best, but Grammy died.

Jake's parents thought maybe he shouldn't stay with Papa this year, but Papa insisted. "Jake and I will be buddies for two weeks."

Jake liked the sound of being buddies with Papa. But he didn't like the thought of Grammy not being there. His parents encouraged him to talk about Grammy, but he didn't know what to say.

As they drove up the long dirt driveway, Papa came out of his old white farmhouse, smiling. He hugged Jake first, then Jake's mom and dad. Then Papa stepped in the house and came out with a puppy—a brown and white English springer spaniel.

"Meet Moses," Papa said. The puppy's whole body wagged. He batted at Jake's socks with his oversized paws and tugged on Jake's shoestrings. Jake rolled him his soccer ball. They became friends instantly.

"Jake, stay away from the creek bank," Mom warned.

"Have fun wading in the creek," Dad told him. "But stay close to Papa."

As his parents got into the car, they both said, "Have a great time!"

Jake waved goodbye. Moses wriggled in his arms and nibbled Jake's nose with tiny needle teeth. Papa put one hand on Jake and one on Moses. "I'm so glad you came!"

Papa took Jake's suitcase to the room full of soccer, football, basketball, and baseball stuff. It had been Jake's mom's room when she was little, but Grammy had made it into a boy's room for him and his brother Ty and cousin Matt, who took their turns visiting each summer.

"Come on," Papa said, walking toward the kitchen. "Dinner's nearly ready."

The smell of spaghetti filled the room. It looked pretty good. But the bread wasn't warm and fresh-baked, and the spaghetti was lumpy. The sauce tasted different, but it had lots of meat. Later Papa took a store-bought apple pie out of the oven. It tasted good, but it wasn't Grammy's pie, the world's best.

Papa asked Jake questions at dinner. But Jake was quiet. After cleaning up, they went into the living room. Papa sat in his big brown recliner, and Jake plopped on the end of the old blue couch.

"You don't seem very happy, Jake," Papa said. "What's wrong?"

Jake hung his head. Finally he asked, "Why did Grammy have to die?"

Papa sighed and propped his hands on his knees. "She's been gone four months. I wake up and reach over, then realize she's not there. Once I had a tooth pulled, and my tongue kept going back to that space. That's how every part of me feels about your grandmother. She's missing, and nothing seems right. After Jesus, she was the best friend I've ever had."

"I know she's in Heaven … but I wish I could bring Grammy back."

Papa walked over and sat by Jake, putting his arm around him. "We both miss her and want to be with her. But if I had the power to bring her back, I wouldn't."

"You wouldn't?"

"Your grandmother's with the most wonderful Person in the universe—Jesus. She doesn't have heart problems or arthritis anymore. Wouldn't it be cruel to bring her back to this world where there's pain and disease and death?"

"I guess so, but ... what's it like where Grammy is?" Jake looked up into Papa's eyes. "Tell me about Heaven."

"Well, Heaven is God's home. And there's only one reliable place to learn about it: God's Book. He wants to leave some surprises for us; so the Bible doesn't tell us everything, but it does say a lot."

"Heaven seems sort of spooky to me," Jake admitted. "I saw a movie about people becoming ghosts when they die. I don't like ghosts, and I don't want to be one. You know my friend Daniel? His sister Lacey died a few months before Grammy. Lacey was only six."

"Your mom mentioned Lacey," Papa said. "She loved Jesus, didn't she?"

Jake nodded.

"Whenever somebody who loves Jesus dies, they leave their bodies here, but I think they walk right into the arms of Jesus in Heaven. Can't you just see Jesus hugging Lacey?"

"I guess so."

"I'm sure He hugged your grandmother too. She probably felt like a little girl again. Jesus was a carpenter, a builder, and He promised He was going to prepare a place for us, a home just right for us. Maybe there's a big sign over Heaven's entrance that says, Welcome Home."

"Samantha Perry says dead people are asleep. Is Grammy sleeping?"

"No, she's wide awake. Samantha may be confused because sometimes the Bible calls dying 'falling asleep,' since dead bodies appear to be sleeping. But the Bible says our spirits go right to Heaven. Do you remember what Jesus told the dying thief on the cross?"

Papa opened his big red Bible, and Jake looked at all the underlines.

Papa pointed to Luke 23. "Jesus said to the thief who repented, '*Today* you will be with me in paradise.' The apostle Paul said that to die is to be with Christ. And to be absent from the body is to be present with the Lord. To be with someone wouldn't mean much if you were sleeping, would it?"

"Then what's Grammy doing?"

Papa turned to Revelation 6:9-11. He read about some people who died, went to Heaven, and talked to God about things on earth. Papa said, "These people are alive and awake, and they're not like ghosts at all. They remember what happened on earth. And they're asking God to do something about it. That means they know about things here, and they're praying to God."

"So when you die ... you don't really die?"

"You die, but that doesn't mean you stop existing or that you fall asleep. It means you go to another place. In Luke 16 Jesus told about a rich man who died and went to Hell, but the man remembered his life on earth and his five brothers. He was sorry about how he'd lived. I expect people in Heaven will remember their lives and families too and be interested in their loved ones."

Papa looked outside. "We've still got an hour's daylight. Let's take a walk."

Jake jumped up. There were lots of great places to go near Papa's house. After they'd walked for ten minutes on a path in the woods, Papa said, "Okay, stay here."

Papa walked off the path twenty feet and stepped behind a thick Douglas fir. Moses was watching a squirrel. When the dog looked back, he cocked his head because, like Jake, he couldn't see Papa.

Jake waited. "Papa? What are you doing?"

Jake stood still, but he couldn't hear anything. Finally Papa stepped out from behind the tree and joined him back on the path. Moses jumped all over him, like he'd been gone a year.

"Okay," Papa asked, "when I went behind the tree, could you see me or hear me?"

"No."

"Then I must have stopped existing, right? Or been sleeping?"

Jake laughed. "No. I knew you were there. I just couldn't see you."

"And we know where Grandma is, even though we can't see her. People's spirits go on living even after their bodies die. Only they're living in a different place where we can't see them. Those in Heaven are very happy, but they're also looking forward to the resurrection, where their spirits will be joined to their bodies again."

They came to a creek, and Jake stuck his hand

into the cold water. "I don't like it when people say, 'I heard you lost your grandma.'"

"Why don't you like that?"

"Because I *didn't* lose her," Jake said, wiping his hand on his jeans. "When you lose something, you don't know where it is. But since we know Grammy's in Heaven, we haven't lost her, have we?"

Papa got quiet. All Jake could hear was the water against the rocks. Finally Papa said, "Here I am trying to teach you about Heaven, and you're teaching me." He put his hand on Jake's shoulder.

"Twenty years ago your grandma went with our pastor's wife to Romania to visit an orphanage. For a whole week she couldn't phone me. I missed her. But I never once said I'd lost her. I knew where she was. I knew who she was with. And even though we couldn't talk to each other, I knew I'd see her again. The same is true now. I know she's in Heaven. I know she's with Jesus, God's people, and angels. I know she's safe and happy in her new home. And I know that eventually I'll join her there."

"If Heaven's our home, does that mean the earth isn't?" Jake asked.

"That's a good question, and the answer is both yes and no," Papa said, eyes smiling. "But it's late. Let's get back to the house and make a fire."

"What about some hot chocolate?"

"That sounds good, doesn't it?" Papa said.

Moses barked and stared up at Papa, who leaned over and patted him on the head.

"Yeah, fella, we'll find a treat for you too."

Now the LORD God had planted a garden in the east, in Eden; and there he put the man he had formed. And the LORD God made all kinds of trees grow out of the ground—trees that were pleasing to the eye and good for food.... A river watering the garden flowed from Eden.... The LORD God took the man and put him in the Garden of Eden to work it and take care of it.

GENESIS 2:8-10,15

Eden

Tuesday morning was bright and sunny. Papa and Jake woke early and made pancakes. Jake put strawberry jam and maple syrup on his. Papa sipped hot coffee; Jake gulped cold milk. Moses ate two pancakes and wanted more.

After grabbing their poles and tackle boxes from the garage, they took Papa's old black Chevy truck to their favorite fishing hole. Moses rode on Jake's lap. He pressed his nose against the window, then licked Jake's face, searching for pancake leftovers. As soon as Papa stopped, Moses jumped out. Stumbling in the tall grass, he proudly led the way.

They put out lawn chairs and cast their lines into the lake. Moses chased a rabbit, but he tripped over himself and somersaulted down the bank. His ears got wet. He shook himself hard. Papa smiled and leaned back in his chair, admiring the yellow and red wildflowers by the lake, the blue sky, and towering green firs. "Breathe that fresh Oregon air. Look at this beautiful world God made."

"Last week Dad read to us about the Garden of Eden," Jake said. "Do you think it was like this?"

"Like this, but far better—countless trees, lots

of fruit, and at least four rivers. There were all kinds of animals, like living in a zoo but without cages. It was completely safe. Tigers next to lambs, goats, and flamingos."

"Animals didn't eat each other?"

"Nope. The Bible says there was no death. I'll bet the colors were fantastic—brighter and bolder than anything here. Maybe some colors we can't even see. No garbage blowing around. Nobody fighting or hurting others."

"But then Adam and Eve disobeyed God," Jake said. "They ate fruit from the tree God said they shouldn't."

Papa nodded. "God made a perfect world. Everything was fresh and exciting. God made people to care for the animals and rule the world. Adam and Eve chose in the place of everyone who lived after them, including you and me. When they sinned against God, it put the whole world under a curse. It damaged everything."

"Then God kicked them out of the Garden." Papa threw back his arm and cast his line in a different place.

"God did that because He's so holy He can't let sinners in His presence. Sometimes people blame God for the bad things that happen in this world, but that's not fair. God gave people freedom to choose. But Adam and Eve made the wrong choice, and we still make wrong choices. So we live under the curse, which includes death and pain and illness."

"Like Grammy's heart disease?"

"That's right. We're not the way God first made us. And the earth isn't the way He first made it. But God promises to make us and the earth perfect again. The whole world will be Eden, but better."

"Better than Eden?"

"In the first few chapters of the Bible paradise was lost because of sin, death, and the curse. In the last few chapters we're told God will do away with all those once and for all. He promises to wipe away every tear when He comes to dwell with His people on the New Earth. In Genesis the devil tempted people; in Revelation he's cast into the lake of fire, never to bother us again. In Eden God blocks the way to the tree of life; in the New Jerusalem the tree of life is available again for everyone. Genesis begins the story on a perfect earth, then shows its ruin. Revelation ends with Christ's return, our resurrection, the judgment, and the New Earth. God promises a new beginning that never ends."

"I'd rather live on earth than in Heaven," Jake said.

"Why?"

"I like animals. And lakes and mountains. I like eating pancakes and strawberry jam and drinking hot chocolate. I like playing with friends and coming to your house in the country and throwing the Frisbee to Moses and reading books."

"God designed you to like earth, Jake. He made the first man directly from the earth. He told the first people their job was to care for the earth, animals, trees, and rivers. God said that the earth and everything He created was very good. So God's happy that you like living here. It's just that this planet has gone wrong. Jesus is a carpenter, and carpenters make things and fix things. Jesus made the universe, and He hasn't given up on it. He's determined to fix it. But the cost of fixing it was terribly high."

"You mean because Jesus had to die on the cross?"

Papa nodded. While both of them were quiet, a fish jumped; they watched the ripples smooth out. "In Sunday school Mrs. Connelly said we won't have bodies in Heaven and that earth isn't our home."

"In the resurrection our spirits will be forever united with our raised bodies, and we'll live on a transformed earth. But earth as it is right now, with sin and death and sorrow, isn't our home. God calls Heaven our home."

Moses looked into the lake, saw a dog's face, and growled. Papa and Jake chuckled. Then Papa leaned close to the water, saw his reflection, and growled. Jake did the same. They laughed at each other's growls.

"Where is Heaven, Papa?"

"Well, Heaven is wherever God's throne is. Tell me, Jake. Who sits on a throne?"

"A king?"

"Right. And who's King of the whole universe?"

"Jesus?"

"Yes. So wherever the throne of Jesus is, that's where Heaven is, right? Right now that throne isn't on earth. But God's going to move his throne and put it somewhere else. Grab my Bible there, by the tackle box. Turn to the end and read Revelation 21:3, about the New Earth."

Jake read the verse, which was underlined with three different colors: "'Now the dwelling of God is with men, and he will live with them. They will be his people, and God himself will be with them and be their God.'"

"Did you catch that, Jake? Three times God promises He'll bring His dwelling down to the New Earth and live with us. Revelation 22 says the throne of God and Jesus will be in the New Jerusalem, the New Earth's capital city. So God will move Heaven down to earth. Then Heaven and earth will be the same place. Ephesians 1:10 says God's plan is 'to bring all things in heaven and on earth together under one head, even Christ.'"

"Will the New Jerusalem cover the whole earth? Will there be other cities too and other places to live? And if it's all city, how could it be like Eden?"

"Good questions," Papa said. "First, the New Jerusalem isn't the only place on the New Earth. Revelation 21 says the kings of earth's nations will travel to the New Jerusalem. So whole countries will exist outside Jerusalem, with many cities and probably lots of open spaces and countryside between those cities. Plenty of room for a natural paradise like Eden."

Jake felt a tug on his line.

"You've got one!" Papa shouted. As Jake reeled the fish in, Moses lunged for it, trying to steal it. Jake pulled it away, but the fish got loose and jumped back in the lake. They laughed.

Jake wasn't sad about losing the fish. The fun had been in catching it. "Papa, I think maybe fish will be happier on the New Earth too!"

Christ Jesus...being in very nature God, did not consider equality with God something to be grasped,
but made himself nothing, taking the very nature of a servant, being made in human likeness.

PHILIPPIANS 3:5-7

CHAPTER THREE

Heaven's Loss

Thursday they slept in. Papa made waffles, and this time Jake only put on Grammy's strawberry jam. Then they headed to one of Jake's favorite places.

"Tell me what was special about Christ's birth," Papa said as they drove east through the Gorge, the Columbia River on their left.

"He was God's Son."

"Right. God made Adam and Eve in His image, knowing that one day His Son would become human. Have you ever thought about what the angels may have felt when God's Son left Heaven? He had always been there. What would it be like without Him? Our gain was Heaven's loss."

"But Jesus went back to Heaven after His resurrection."

"True. But God becoming a man changed everything. Jesus will remain human forever. He'll always have a resurrected human body suited for life on earth. Scripture says He'll bring Heaven down to the New Earth where He'll reign as King of Kings. And we'll be kings and queens ruling under Him."

"And my friend Jimmy won't be in a wheelchair."

"And your Uncle Tommy's mind will work

right. In our resurrection bodies, we'll be who God created us to be. I'll be myself, but without the bad parts. No sin or bad attitudes or aching back or high blood pressure. You'll be Jake, but Jake made perfect."

"We'll really be ourselves?"

"Who else would we be?" Papa smiled, taking the exit. "Job said, 'In my flesh I will see God … I, and not another.' After His resurrection Jesus said to His disciples, 'Look at my hands and my feet. It is I myself! Touch me and see; a ghost does not have flesh and bones, as you see I have.' Jesus called people in Heaven by name, including Lazarus. He says on the New Earth we'll eat with Abraham, Isaac, and Jacob. He called them by their earthly names because in Heaven they're the same people they were on earth, but perfect. Remember when Moses and Elijah appeared with Christ on that mountain? They were the real Moses and Elijah. And you'll be the real Jake."

From the Multnomah Falls parking lot, they walked through a tunnel under train tracks. When they came out, Jake looked way up at the top of the falls. "Are we going to hike up there, like we did last summer?"

"If you want to," Papa said.

"I do!" Jake shouted, running ahead of Papa.

They stopped to catch their breath on the bridge partway up the trail and gazed down at water crashing on rocks.

"Samantha said when we go to Heaven, we won't remember what happened on earth," Jake said.

"The Bible says we'll all stand before God and tell Him about our lives on earth. That means we'll have better memories, not worse. To praise God for His mighty works here, we'll have to remember our lives here, won't we?"

"Samantha also said people become angels when they die."

"The Bible says angels are 'ministering spirits sent to serve those who will inherit salvation.' Angels serve us, but angels and people are very different. People will always be people. Angels will always be angels."

"Are angels all alike?"

"They all share things in common. But like

people, they're individuals—like Michael and Gabriel with their own personalities and names and jobs. Michael, the archangel or chief angel, serves under God; the other angels serve God under Michael. Angels that we can't see protect and serve *us* all the time. The Bible says one day we'll be in charge of angels. Won't it be fun to meet in Heaven angels who've watched over us? And to find out their names and the people they were assigned to before us?"

Jake looked around at the waterfall and rocks and trees and felt the wind blowing his hair. *Are angels here right now?* he wondered.

As they started up the trail again, Jake asked, "Papa, on the New Earth, will Mom still be a woman? And will Dad still be a man?"

"Sure. After His resurrection Jesus was a man, just like before. We'll always be human; so our bodies will always be male or female."

Four people dressed in colorful outfits passed them on the trail.

"Will people wear different clothes in Heaven?" Jake asked.

"Well, the Bible describes people in Heaven wearing white robes. White meant they were clean. But in Bible times robes are what most people wore every day. So maybe we'll wear clothes like we wear now."

"Jeans? T-shirts? Tennis shoes?"

"Maybe. Those would be just as normal for us as robes and sandals were for first-century people."

"Will we ever have to dress up?"

"I like wearing the kind of clothes I have on right now. But it's nice to dress up sometimes too! There may be special events, celebrations to dress up for. You like parties, don't you?"

"Usually. But at Brady's party, I didn't know

anybody. And Brady made fun of me."

"There won't be any loneliness or hurt feelings in Heaven. Everybody'll be friendly. Nobody'll be left out. Jesus will be the center of everything. He'll be pleased with us. We'll be delighted with Him. We'll worship Him, talk with Him, and laugh with Him."

"Laugh with Jesus? Really?"

"Sure! God created laughter. He gave us a sense of humor because He has one." Papa stopped, wiped his forehead, and caught his breath. "When we visit the zoo, we'll see the otters. God designed them to play all day so they could have a good time and He could enjoy watching them."

"Otters make me laugh," Jake said.

"That means God makes you laugh, because He's the one who created otters with those funny qualities. It makes God happy to hear you laugh because He made the joke, and you got it! Think about aardvarks and baboons, giraffes, a cat chasing a ball, or Moses growling at his reflection. God wants us to laugh. Don't you think Jesus laughed with His disciples?"

"I never thought about it."

"Jesus said, 'Blessed are you who weep now, for you will laugh.' That's a promise of laughter in Heaven. Jesus also said, 'leap for joy, because great is your reward in heaven.' Can you picture someone leaping for joy without laughing? I think Jesus might have the biggest laugh on the New Earth!"

Panting, they finally made it to the top of the trail. They looked way down to the bridge, the lodge, people looking like ants, and the Columbia River. Papa took out his binoculars and kept showing things to Jake. After a while Jake stepped back. The view was awesome but a little scary.

While they rested, they ate apples and granola bars and drank from their water bottles. On the hike back down, they stepped off the trail to look at a patch of reddish flowers Papa called columbine. Jake watched a pair of hawks fly in lazy circles. "You're sure the New Earth will be as good as all this?"

"Far better. We've never seen God's earth in all its glory. We've never seen animals as they were before Adam and Eve sinned. We've never seen people like God intended them to be. We live in earth's ruins. And if it can be so beautiful now, imagine how amazing it will be when God changes it to its original glory!"

Jake smiled wide. He leaned forward on the trail; then his feet ran to catch up with his body. He called back to Papa, "It'll be fun to go exploring. And have banquets. And laugh!"

Papa moved quickly to catch up. Jake remembered when Papa used to be faster than him.

When they got back down to the bridge, feeling the spray of water cooling their faces, Papa said, "When we explore and eat and laugh, it'll always make us think about God. We'll thank Him constantly. We'll worship Him because He gives us every pleasure. That's true now, but in Heaven we'll realize it every moment. And we'll never be disappointed because God and Heaven will always be better than we expect. The Bible says God will do way more than all we can ask or imagine."

Papa took Jake into the lodge for a late lunch. Before eating, Papa said, "Let's thank God for the beauty of this world and for the spectacular beauty that we'll experience when we live with Jesus on the New Earth."

They bowed their heads, and both prayed. At the end Jake added, "And, Lord, thanks for ice cream too."

When he looked up, Papa smiled. "Okay. After lunch we'll have ice cream."

There was a violent earthquake, for an angel of the Lord came down from heaven and, going to the tomb, rolled back the stone and sat on it....The angel said to the women, "Do not be afraid, for I know that you are looking for Jesus, who was crucified. He is not here; he has risen, just as he said."

MATTHEW 28:2, 5-6

CHAPTER FOUR

Out of the Tomb

On a rainy Saturday afternoon they sat in Papa's office. He had books everywhere, all the books by C. S. Lewis and hundreds more.

"You read a lot, don't you, Papa?"

"I sure do. God gave us the gift of language and curious minds; so we love to learn. I like a good movie, and games are fun, but I'll take reading good books—especially God's Book—over television or movies or video games any day. These books help me learn about God." He pointed to the shelf. "Pick out one of the Narnia books, and we'll read it together."

After chicken salad sandwiches, Papa and Jake read—Papa in his recliner, Jake on the couch with Moses beside him, pressing his snout against a page and making Jake laugh. Papa and Jake each read the same chapter from their own copies of *The Horse and His Boy.* They talked about it when they were done. Then they read the next chapter and talked some more. It was a fun way to read.

When they were halfway through the book, Papa said, "Are you as tired of my cooking as I am? Let's drive into town for dinner."

Jake didn't mind Papa's cooking, but he didn't try to talk him out of the trip. They stood for a moment on the porch and listened to the rain pound. It sounded wonderful. Then they ran to the truck and drove to a restaurant called Mattie's where there were people of all different sizes, shapes, and colors—some speaking with accents.

"We didn't used to have so many different people in this area," Papa said. "God made each of us, and I think it makes Him happy for us all to gather in the same place."

After they ordered, Jake asked, "Will we all look alike in Heaven?"

"I'm sure we won't. The Bible says Heaven's filled with people of every tribe, nation, and language. Each snowflake's unique, and so is each person. God makes us different because He likes us that way."

"I'd be a better basketball player if I were taller."

"Maybe, but you wouldn't be as good at something else. Maybe some people will be bigger or some smaller on the New Earth, but we'll all be healthy, untouched by disease or disabilities or accidents."

"Mom looks in the mirror sometimes and says she wishes she looked different."

Papa chuckled. "Well, on the New Earth, no matter what we look like, our bodies will be pleasing to God, ourselves, and each other. Nobody'll wish for a different nose or ears or teeth. We won't try to hide or show off or remake ourselves. We'll be beautiful without trying because God will make us just like He wants, and He's the master Artist."

Jake took a big bite of toasted cheese sandwich, his favorite, and then drank some orange juice. "Will we really eat and drink in Heaven?"

"Sure. Remember, we'll have real human bodies. The Bible speaks often of eating and feasts, not only on this earth but on the New Earth. Feasting means eating and all that goes with it—celebrations and fun, conversations, storytelling, and hanging out with those we love."

"And laughing," Jake reminded him.

"Right. People who love each other love to laugh while they eat together. Jesus promised His disciples that they would sit at His table and eat and drink with Him in His kingdom."

"Will there be toasted cheese sandwiches? Cookie-dough ice cream?"

Papa laughed. "I don't know, but for sure the

food on the New Earth will taste better with our resurrected taste buds!"

Papa looked at Jake. "Close your eyes and imagine Jesus walking out of that tomb that first Easter morning, angels bowing at His greatness."

Jake closed his eyes.

"His risen body was the same body that died. It had the marks from the nails on hands and feet to prove it. After His resurrection, Jesus fixed breakfast for His disciples. He ate it with them. He proved He had a real human body and that resurrected people *can* and *do* eat real food. Maybe you've never yet tasted your favorite food. The Bible talks about people coming from all over to sit and eat together in Heaven. It speaks of the great wedding feast. Think about it, Jake. What does our family do when we gather for Thanksgiving and Christmas?"

"We always eat!"

"And do we just eat crackers and celery?"

"No. We eat big meals. And Grandma's apple pie." Jake's face fell.

"That's okay, Jake. Grammy would *love* for you to talk about her apple pie." They were both quiet while Papa paid the bill. He left a generous tip and told Jake that's what Christians should do since they're supposed to be like Jesus, and He's the most generous giver of all.

They climbed into the truck and pulled out on the road. Papa glanced at Jake. "I'll bet Grammy will bake apple pies on the New Earth, and we'll eat them!"

"Really?"

"I don't see why not. Revelation 22 says there'll be fruit on the New Earth—twelve different kinds of fruit from the tree of life alone. We know we'll eat, and Scripture says that people will be serving God and each other. So can you think of any good reason Grammy wouldn't serve us her apple pie?"

"No. And maybe Jesus will eat it too."

"Yes. He promised He'd eat with us in Heaven. Think how happy Grammy would be to share her pie with Jesus. And imagine how much Jesus would enjoy it—every bite. I can just see the look on her face when He tells her how good it is!"

Papa cleared his throat and was quiet for the last few minutes of the drive.

When they came in the front door, Moses shivered with happiness. After running around outside, then sliding across the kitchen's tile floor, he jumped into Jake's lap and plopped his head on his legs, staying perfectly still except for his wagging tail.

Jake turned to Papa. "Jesus dematerialized in His resurrection body, didn't He?"

"You mean like in Star Trek?" Papa laughed. "Well, somehow He came through a locked door to the apostles. And Luke says He disappeared from the sight of two disciples at Emmaus. And when Jesus left the earth, He rose to Heaven, defying gravity. Maybe those were things only He can do. Or maybe our bodies will do them too. Maybe we'll be able to fly like birds or dive deep like whales and hold our breath for hours. Or turn corners in space and travel light years away in an instant."

"Fun!" Jake exclaimed.

"We don't know for sure, but whatever it's like, life after the resurrection will be awesome!"

As they finished up their day over mugs of hot chocolate, Papa sighed. "Every year that goes by, as my body and mind get older, I look forward more and more to being with Jesus, then eventually the resurrection."

"But you can still hike to the top of the falls, Papa."

"I'm very grateful for that. But my body's slowing down. And that's okay. I plan to do plenty of hiking on the New Earth."

Jake thought of a question he'd been wanting to ask. "Will Lacey be six years old forever?"

"I don't think so. Just like your grandmother won't be seventy years old forever. Our age when we die doesn't matter; in the resurrection God can make us any way He wants."

"Lacey's parents were awfully sad when she died."

"Sure they were. But you know what? Maybe in the resurrection, Lacey will start at the same age she died and then finish growing up on the New Earth. It would be just like God to do that. I think on the New Earth many opportunities lost in this life will be given to us again. Parents whose hearts were broken by their children's deaths will be with them again—we know that for sure. And maybe they'll have the joy of seeing those children grow up in a perfect world."

"Will some people look older than others?"

"We might all have the bodies of twenty-five-year-olds. Or maybe when I look at you, Jake, you'll seem younger, and when you look at me, I'll seem older." He pointed at an old family photograph on the wall, from when he was a child. "And when I look at my parents, they might seem older to me, and I might seem younger to them. But in our hearts all of us will be young. Jesus said we must become like children to enter God's kingdom." Papa looked at his watch. "It's getting late. Tomorrow I'm going to ask you to tell me the very best thing about Heaven. Sleep on it, okay?"

As he lay in his bed, just before he went to sleep and dreamed a great dream, Jake thought about feasts and adventures and explorations. And he wondered how to answer Papa's question.

Blessed are you when people insult you, persecute you and falsely say all kinds of evil against you because of me. Rejoice and be glad, because great is your reward in heaven.

MATTHEW 5:11 - 12

CHAPTER FIVE

Safely Home

*I*t was Sunday morning. Sunshine streamed through the kitchen window. "I'm not tired of waffles yet," Jake told Papa. "Neither is Moses."

Later, at church, the pastor talked about the greatest commandments: loving God with all your heart and loving your neighbor as yourself.

Church people told Jake he'd grown a lot since last summer. He was embarrassed but glad they remembered him and noticed he was taller.

Afterward they had a picnic behind the church building, with volleyball and softball. Jake kicked a soccer ball with two boys his age. Then they went over to somebody's house and threw Frisbees and explored the woods. When Jake and Papa drove home, it was late, and the stars were bright.

Jake let Moses out while Papa found the flashlight. He led them to their special place near the creek where there were big rocks to sit on and a clear view of the sky. Moses settled on Jake's lap. Papa pointed up and told Jake about the stars, calling dozens of them by name.

"Abraham Lincoln said he didn't understand how people could look at the stars and not believe in God. I don't understand it either." Papa was silent for a moment. Then he turned to Jake. "I told you I'd ask you what the most important thing about Heaven is.

What's your answer?"

Jake looked at the sky. "That God lives there?"

"Exactly! It's always about God, isn't it? God's full of joy, and Heaven's full of God. Heaven is the overflow of God's joy. When people love sports, games, books, movies, and food, they may not know it, but they're really loving God because He's the source of all joy. God's greatest gift to us is Himself. We were made for a Person and a place. Jesus is the Person. Heaven is the place."

That moment the sky lit up.

"Wow," Jake cried, startling Moses. "Did you see that?"

"A double meteor!" Papa said. "Look! Two doubles in a row!"

They sat quietly, not wanting to miss anything. Finally Papa said, "Wasn't that kind of God to remind us right then that He's with us? Revelation 22 says on the New Earth we will see God's face. That's the greatest thing any of us will ever experience, Jake. Far greater than a double meteor or supernova."

"To see Jesus is to see God, right?"

"Right. One of Christ's names is Immanuel, which means 'God with us.' Jesus said, 'Anyone who has seen me has seen the Father.' So when we see Jesus in Heaven, *we will see God*. Won't that be awesome?"

Jake nodded.

"Think of the stories Jesus will tell us: about creating the world and distant galaxies, what the universe is like a billion light years away, about making the first dinosaur, becoming an unborn baby, growing up, and healing people. Wouldn't you like to spend an evening with Jesus? A year? Well, He says we can live with Him forever! That's really exciting to me, because Jesus is my Savior, and He's also my best friend."

Jake stared at the stars, which seemed to get brighter by the minute. Papa pointed out the stars that formed the great square of Pegasus the horse, including one called Alpheratz, head of the constellation Andromeda. Then he helped Jake follow from star to star until Jake saw a little fuzzy football-shaped glow, which was clearer when he looked at it out the corner of his eye.

"What is it, Papa?"

"That's the Great Galaxy of Andromeda. Using a star chart, I found it in the sky by myself when I was your age. It's a galaxy much bigger than our Milky

Way, containing billions of stars. And it's two and a half million light years away. Think of it, Jake. Light's so fast it travels seven and a half times around the earth in a second." Papa snapped his fingers. "But the Andromeda galaxy's so far away that if it blacked out right now, we'd still see it for two and a half million years. It's the farthest you can see with the naked eye. Most people don't know where to look. So right now you're seeing farther than most people ever have."

Jake couldn't take his eyes off it. They sat there a long time. When Papa asked if he was ready to go in, Jake didn't answer. He was lost in Andromeda.

Finally they walked back to the house. Papa took his telescope out of the garage and set it up on the grass. He pointed it at the Andromeda galaxy. Jake studied it a long time. Then they looked at Jupiter and counted four of its moons. Finally Papa pointed the telescope at Saturn.

"I see the rings!" Jake exclaimed. Moses kept trying to jump up until Jake held his face up to the eyepiece. Jake and Papa laughed hard.

Clouds started coming in, and the wind picked up. "Storm's coming," Papa announced. "Time for hot chocolate!"

They went into Papa's office, mugs warming their hands. Papa showed Jake a beautiful big photograph of several hundred galaxies called the Hubble Deep Field.

"See the spiral and elliptical galaxies—and all these other shapes and colors?" Papa pointed from galaxy to galaxy. "There are hundreds of millions of stars in each of these galaxies, and it's just a tiny portion of God's universe. There are more stars in the universe than grains of sand on earth, more galaxies than blades of grass. When I look at the Great Galaxy of Andromeda and the Orion Nebula in the winter, I worship God. They remind me of how powerful He is because Psalm 8 calls them the work of God's fingers. It's okay that I'm so small and can't control much because He's way bigger than the universe He created, and He can control everything. And He loves us so much, He sent Jesus to save us so we could live with Him forever."

They went to the living room, and Jake sat down by Papa's big red Bible with gold-edged pages. "Jake, I quoted from Job 19 the other day. I'd like you to read verses 25 to 27."

Jake opened Papa's Bible and read, "'I know that

my Redeemer lives, and that in the end he will stand upon the earth. And after my skin has been destroyed, yet in my flesh I will see God; I myself will see him with my own eyes—I, and not another. How my heart yearns within me!'"

"What do you think that means, Jake?"

"Is he talking about Jesus?"

"Yes! Job wrote two thousand years before Jesus came. But he said his Redeemer, the Messiah, was alive even then. Jesus was born and died and rose and went back to Heaven, but one day He'll return to earth. Job says his skin will be destroyed, and yet in his flesh he'll see God. That means he'll die; his body will be destroyed. Yet one day he'll have that same body again. What's he talking about?"

"The resurrection?"

"And what does Job say he's going to see with his own eyes, in his resurrection body?"

Jake looked at the Bible. "He says, 'I will see God. I myself will see him with my own eyes.' Will it be scary to see God, Papa?"

"Well, the Bible says, 'no one can see God and live.' If we were still sinners, it would be very scary to see God, because His absolute holiness would destroy us. But when we meet Jesus face to face, we won't be sinners anymore. The Bible says we'll be holy; we'll have the righteousness of Christ Himself. So we'll fall on our knees at His greatness, but we'll rejoice to see God in all His holiness and love. That's what Job says he longs for. That's what I long for too."

"But we can't see God now, right?"

"Not directly. But read Romans 1:20."

Jake turned to Romans and read, "'For since the creation of the world God's invisible qualities—his eternal power and divine nature—have been clearly seen, being understood from what has been made.'"

"That means we can see God's qualities and greatness in His creation," Papa said, "like the stars and galaxies, animals, forests, and oceans. And we can see Him in people too because people are made in God's image. So when your parents, friends, teachers, or coaches show you love, you see Jesus in them."

"But in Heaven we'll see Jesus face to face, right?"

"Right. God has shown me grace all my life, Jake. He's been with me in good times and bad. I'm so grateful. I say thanks to Jesus often throughout the day. But I can't wait to thank Him face to face in Heaven."

Jake raised his eyes to Papa. "Lacey and Grammy are seeing Jesus now. And they're okay, aren't they?"

"They're more than okay. They're fantastic! You know, most of the apostles were killed because they spoke up for Jesus. Christians are still persecuted in many countries. I think about what it must be like when they die and meet Jesus. Their life journey may be difficult, but He brings every one of them safely home. Imagine Jesus stepping down from His throne in Heaven and embracing them. Imagine the chains of this life falling to the floor. Imagine being freed and healed, never to be imprisoned or sick or hurt again. Then imagine Jesus saying, 'Well done, my good and faithful servant; enter into your master's joy.' I think about that every day, Jake. I hope you'll think about it too."

Jake nodded.

"Let's thank God for who He is and what He's done for us. Okay?"

They got down on their knees next to each other, hands propped on the couch, with Moses nestled between them.

Papa prayed, "Thank You, Jesus, for making the universe—the stars, earth, animals, and people.

Thank You for my grandson Jake. I'm so happy that he loves You. And that his brother Ty and parents, and aunt, uncle, and cousins Matt and Jack do too. Thank You for letting him come each summer to visit. Even though we miss his grandmother, thank You that she's happy and healthy now and that we'll see her again soon."

Jake prayed, "Jesus, thanks for church today and my new friends. And thanks for making Jupiter and its moons and Saturn and its rings, and especially the Andromeda galaxy. I can't believe I got to see something so far away! I pray for Christians who are persecuted. Help them know You love them. And remind them that one day You'll welcome them into Heaven."

After they prayed, they sat on the floor and played with Moses. Then Papa asked Jake, "How about some popcorn, with butter?"

"Yeah!"

I confer on you a kingdom, just as my Father conferred one on me, so that you may eat and
drink at my table in my kingdom and sit on thrones.

CHAPTER SIX

Heaven's Table

*T*uesday Papa and Jake picked strawberries for three hours. Grammy always made jam and gave it away. Today they took the fresh-picked berries to needy people in the community. Jake felt good about his hard work after he saw how happy they were to get the berries.

They stopped for burgers at Dea's, Papa's favorite hangout. Jake asked, "What kind of place will Heaven be?"

"It'll be a whole universe—the New Heavens and the New Earth, this planet made perfect. Heaven's also called a 'better country' in Hebrews 11. What can you tell me about countries?"

"They have land and rulers and citizens. And maybe kings."

"Yes. And cities. Jesus said His faithful disciples will rule over five or ten cities. King Jesus will have His throne in the New Jerusalem. What do you know about cities?"

"They have lots of big buildings."

"Revelation 21 says the kings of the nations of the New Earth will bring their treasures into the New Jerusalem."

"What kind of treasures?"

"Probably art, crafts, musical instruments, food, clothes, jewelry. I think we'll bring things we make

and offer them to our King, like Christmas pres-
ents we give to Jesus. When He sees them, He'll be
pleased. We'll probably share them with each other
too. Showing love to God and our neighbors isn't just
something we're supposed to do now. We're going to
be doing it forever!"

"What will the New Jerusalem be like?"

"The Bible says there'll be a big river flowing
through the city center, with the tree of life on both
sides. Maybe that'll be the New Eden, a huge Paradise
Park. But … you don't look very excited, Jake."

"Cities can be dirty and crowded. And there's
crime."

"Not in that city! It'll have all the good things
about cities with none of the bad. Jesus will be
there, and He'll be King! And everyone will be your
friend."

"Will we meet people talked about in the Bible?"

"Sure. I want to meet Abraham, David, Ruth,
Esther, Peter, and Paul. And people in history like
John Newton, who wrote 'Amazing Grace.' And
William Wilberforce, who spent his whole life fighting
to stop the slave trade. And Nate Saint, the missionary
pilot. Won't it be fun having dinner with them?"

"We'll really do that?"

"The Bible says so. It talks about eating with
Abraham, Isaac, and Jacob at great feasts. I picture
Abraham Lincoln serving a meal to a woman who was
once a slave. And maybe a knight from the Middle
Ages—a man who loved Jesus—will sit down next to
a boy like you and tell him exciting stories. Maybe
angels who guarded us on earth
will stand by us as we eat.
And at last we'll be
able to see them!"

"Cool," Jake said.

After lunch they
went to the high
school tennis court.
They tried to see how
many balls in a row they
could hit.

Later as they drove away,
Jake talked excitedly. "That was fun. I
like tennis!"

"It's great playing sports, isn't it?"

Jake suddenly got quiet. Finally he asked, "Papa,
will Heaven be boring?"

"Boring? Never! Humans didn't invent fun, activity, and pleasure. God did. King David said to God, 'In your presence there is fullness of joy; at your right hand are pleasures forevermore.' God is endlessly fascinating; so Heaven will be endlessly fascinating."

"But what will we do?"

"We'll worship God in everything—singing, playing, talking, eating, traveling, exploring, relaxing. God says we'll serve Him forever. You'll have a job, Jake, and you'll love it. I've read hundreds of books. Someday I'd like to write one—maybe about God's greatness, as seen in the wonders of distant planets."

Jake saw a far-off look in his grandfather's eyes.

As they pulled up to the house, rain started pouring. They ran inside and minutes later lightning and thunder surrounded them. Jake loved storms, as long as he was safe and dry. They watched through the living room windows.

"That's quite a fireworks display God's putting on for us," Papa said.

As the storm continued, Jake asked, "Papa, do you think we'll read books in Heaven?"

"I do. God invented language. He made us with a love of storytelling. The Bible's sixty-six books will last forever. God says in the book of Malachi that a scroll of remembrance is being written in Heaven now about the works of God's faithful people on earth. Maybe angels are writing about you and me, Jake. And if it's being written in Heaven, doesn't that mean it'll be read in Heaven? With all that'll happen forever in the New Universe, there'll certainly be plenty of new things to write and read about too!"

"Will there be plays and movies?"

"Some people love to perform. Others are writers, some are directors, and others like building sets. We all enjoy a good drama. It's part of our God-given creativity. It's part of using our gifts and enjoying each other and our Lord. Would there have been music and art and drama without that first sin? Sure, and it all would have been much better. God built us to live in relationships with each other. Stories and entertainment that honor God are part of the life He always intended for us. So there's every reason to believe they'll be part of our lives on the New Earth."

Jake slowly asked a question, like he was afraid the answer would be no. "Will we play tennis on the New Earth? And soccer? And basketball?"

"The Bible doesn't tell us, but I think the answer's yes. See, God made us like Himself, with a love for play. He gave us minds and wills to invent games. In Scripture God compares the Christian life to sporting events. He wouldn't do that if sports were evil. If people hadn't become sinners, I'm sure they still would have invented sports. Nobody will have a bad attitude there; so sports will always be fun and healthy and God-glorifying."

"One of the boys I played with after church can't walk," Jake said.

"That's Gabe. He plays wheelchair basketball."

"But he'd like to run and jump."

"Yes, he would. And he's going to. Gabe knows Jesus. On the New Earth our resurrection bodies won't have disabilities. Gabe will run and jump as much as he wants to."

Jake smiled broadly. "Will there be computers on the New Earth?"

"I wouldn't be surprised. Technology helps us rule the earth as God commanded. He created natural laws and gave us minds for math and science so we can figure out how to make things better. So what should we expect on the New Earth? Not only trees and rivers and animals—God's creations—but also human creations. Jesus designed us to make things and fix things, like He did as a carpenter. We could make tables, chairs, cabinets, machinery, technology. If people had never sinned, wouldn't they have invented the wheel? Sure. In the world as it is now, computers and the Internet can be used for good and for bad. But in Heaven there won't be any more bad. Everything will be good. On the New Earth I expect we'll always be inventing new things to care for God's creation and show off His greatness."

"Will there be cars? Planes? Spaceships?"

Papa laughed. "The Bible doesn't tell us that either. But it says the New Jerusalem will have streets and gates for coming and going. Will we ride bikes? Soar outside the city in helicopters or airplanes? Who knows? But traveling helps us manage and explore God's creation in order to learn more about Him. So why not?"

After they finished a late dinner, the sky cleared. Jake wanted to see Saturn's rings again; so Papa set up his telescope. Then they walked back to their favorite place on the big rocks by the stream and gazed up at the night sky. They saw meteors again.

"Since there'll be a New Earth," Jake asked, "will there be a New Saturn?"

"God promises to make not only a New Earth but also New Heavens. That's everything in the sky—the entire universe. Including that place right there." Papa pointed.

"The Great Galaxy of Andromeda," Jake said, wonder in his voice.

"Since it's part of God's original creation, I think the Bible's promise of New Heavens means there'll be a new Andromeda galaxy." There in the darkness, it was like Papa had a light on his face. "You know, ever since that night I first saw it, I've dreamed of going there. Maybe one day I will."

"You really think so? In a space ship?"

"Or maybe there will be other ways to get there. I'm not sure. But the heavens declare God's glory even now. Won't the New Heavens do that even more? Exploring the New Heavens could help us learn more about God and praise Him for His power

and creative genius. Maybe one day you and I will write a song about God's glory shown in the New Andromeda Galaxy!"

"That would be so cool," Jake said.

"And who knows what else? Maybe we'll time-travel and study earth's history from a front-row seat. Maybe we'll see how our small acts of kindness changed others' lives."

"Like giving away those strawberries this morning?"

"Exactly! Ephesians 2:7 says that in the coming ages God will be revealing to us the riches of His grace and kindness to us. That means we'll always be learning more about Him. And because He's infinite, there'll always be more for us to learn."

Papa put his arm around Jake as they looked at the stars.

Jake pointed to that little blur left of the great square of Pegasus. "Papa, if you ever travel to the New Andromeda Galaxy … can I go with you?"

In the same way, I tell you, there is rejoicing in the presence of
the angels of God over one sinner who repents.

LUKE 15:10

CHAPTER SEVEN

Heaven's Balcony

Saturday morning Jake and Papa watched on television the Wimbledon tennis championships. Papa offered to make an omelet like Grammy used to. But Jake knew Papa was better at waffles than anything; so they had waffles with strawberries again. At Wimbledon people were eating strawberries too.

"Can Grammy hear what we're saying right now?" Jake asked when the match was over.

"That's a good question. Remember those people in Heaven spoken of in Revelation 6? They realized what was happening on earth. God's great plan of redemption is being worked out here and now. I think it's like center court at Wimbledon. Everybody's watching."

"Papa ... is it okay for me to talk to Grammy?"

"Well, you shouldn't ask her to talk to *you*. The Bible tells us not to do that. But you can talk to Jesus any time you want. And if you want Grammy to know something, I think Jesus would be happy to tell her for you. That's up to Him. Remember, though, if you do that, you're praying to God, not to your grandma."

Jake nodded. "When we die, will we remember where we lived and what we did and who we knew? Will I remember you, Papa?"

"Sure! Scripture says the New Earth will have memorials about the tribes of Israel and the apostles. Jesus promised that in Heaven those who endured bad things on earth will be comforted. Christians who were killed by bad people remember their troubles on earth, but God comforts them and gives them joy."

"When we were climbing at Multnomah Falls, you said we'd have better memories in Heaven, right? So we won't forget our family and friends? Or pets and school and playing ball?"

"The Bible says we'll give an account of our lives on earth, including things we've forgotten now. To do that we'll have to have great memories, won't we? Sure, once we're in Heaven, in one sense we'll forget about our worries. We won't feel depressed and guilty about bad choices we made, because we'll know Christ has forgiven us. But every day of our lives here we should be learning lessons about Christ and His love and grace. We'll never forget those lessons, Jake. Much of this life carries right over to the next life. We'll never forget the wonderful ways God took care of us. Remember how Christ's resurrection body had nail scars in His hands and feet?"

"Won't it make us sad to see them?"

"Those scars will always remind us how much Jesus loves us. He doesn't want us to forget, and we won't want to. Heaven isn't about not knowing and not remembering. It's about seeing things through God's eyes and experiencing His joy."

"When Grammy died," Jake said, "I was afraid she'd forget me."

"Never," Papa said, wiping his eyes. He opened his Bible and read in 1 Thessalonians 4 that God wants His people to know about those who've died and gone to Heaven. "God says He doesn't want us 'to grieve like the rest of men, who have no hope.' He goes on to say 'we will be with the Lord forever. Therefore encourage each other with these words.'"

"I felt really bad when Grammy died," Jake said.

"Me too. It's right to feel bad. Jesus cried about the death of His friend Lazarus. But God says our grief is *different* from those who have no hope of seeing their loved ones again. Your relationship with your grandma didn't end, Jake. It was interrupted. She got there first, but we're going to the same place—Heaven. I'm going to join her there.

Someday you'll join both of us. So will your mom and dad and brother and cousins. Then we'll always be together with the Lord, and we'll be with Him when He brings His throne to the New Earth. I can't think of a more wonderful promise. Can you?"

Jake couldn't.

They went for a hike around the lake, weaving through trees, listening to frogs and watching owls, squirrels, and rabbits. They stood quietly twenty feet from two deer, until Moses barked like crazy, and the deer bolted. Papa and Jake came to a stream, then sat down, and drank cold water from it.

"Papa, how can we be sure we'll go to Heaven when we die?"

"The Bible tells us in First John, 'I write these things to you who believe in the name of the Son of God so that *you may know that you have eternal life*.' We don't have to guess or hope. We can know for sure, if we trust Jesus for our salvation. Unfortunately, many people just assume they're going to Heaven without Jesus."

"Why?"

"Maybe they think they're good enough. Nobody wants to believe he's going to Hell. But Hell is real. Jesus said more about it than anybody else in Scripture. He said, 'Enter through the narrow gate. For wide is the gate and broad is the road that leads to destruction, and many enter through it. But small is the gate and narrow the road that leads to life, and only a few find it.' Here's one of the first verses I ever memorized: 'All have sinned and fall short of the glory of God.' Do you know what that means?"

"We don't deserve to go to Heaven?"

"Exactly. God's completely good, but sometimes we think and do bad things, don't we? This breaks our relationship with God. He had to do something to change us, to make us holy enough to enter His presence. Jesus took our death sentence on Himself so that we don't have to go to Hell, but can live forever with Him in Heaven."

"Sometimes ... that's hard to understand."

"I have an idea. How about after dinner we watch *The Lion, the Witch and the Wardrobe*?"

Jake nodded eagerly.

Later they ate popcorn as they watched the movie. They'd both seen it before, but it was fun watching it together.

Afterward Papa asked Jake, "Did Edmund deserve to die?"

"The witch thought so. And Aslan agreed, didn't he?"

"Yes. That was the law; traitors had to die. And Edmund was a traitor to Peter, Susan, Lucy, the Beavers, and everybody—especially Aslan. Edmund was guilty and deserved to die. Was there anything Edmund could do to save himself from death?"

Jake shook his head.

"Then how was he saved?"

"Aslan died in his place. On the stone table."

"In the real world, do you see why Christ's death on the cross was necessary to save all of us, including *you*, Jake? On the one hand, you're a good boy. You know how much God loves you and how much your parents and I love you, don't you? But the truth is, you're not always good. You're not perfect. You've inherited sin that goes all the way back to Adam. And you're guilty of your own sins—wrong thoughts and attitudes and actions. Isn't that true?"

"Yes," Jake said, squirming.

"I'm a sinner too. Like Edmund, I deserve to die for my sins. Do you see that you deserve to die for your sins too?"

Jake nodded. "I think so."

"Edmund couldn't do anything to be saved from death but be sorry for his sins and accept Aslan's sacrifice for him. When he did, he was forgiven and became a new person." Papa looked at his watch. "Well, it's time for bed, but first I'm going to read to you Romans 3:21-25. See if it reminds you of *The Lion, the Witch and the Wardrobe*."

Papa read it to Jake. It did remind him of the Narnia story.

Papa quoted Jesus: "'I am the way and the truth and the life. No one comes to the Father except through me.'" Then he explained, "That means Jesus is the only way to get to Heaven. Jesus says, 'Whoever is thirsty, let him come; and whoever wishes, let him take the free gift of the water of life.' The gift is free for us. But it cost Jesus His life. He rose from the grave, defeating sin and death. By trusting Him, we can live with Him forever. You accepted Jesus as your Savior years ago, right?"

Jake nodded. "When I was six."

"I gave my life to Jesus when I was fifteen. Jesus

said that whenever a sinner turns *away* from sin and turns *to* God, there's rejoicing in the presence of the angels of Heaven. That means that the angels and those who live with them rejoice when people on earth get right with Jesus. It's like they're looking over a balcony to see what's going on here, and when they see us follow God, they get excited!"

"Grammy too?"

"She's there where Jesus and the angels are, and I'll bet she's watching right now. I know she's proud of you, Jake, and very happy to see you follow Jesus. Why don't we get on our knees here by the sofa and thank God for saving us?"

They thanked God for Jake's parents and brother and cousins, for the Narnia stories, for Grammy, and for Jesus dying on the cross so they could go to Heaven instead of Hell. Jake asked Jesus to give Grammy a hug for him. Papa did too.

"I think those prayers made Jesus happy, Jake. And I'll bet He's hugging your grandma right now." As Jake climbed into bed, Papa said, "All right, let's get a good night's sleep because tomorrow we—"

"We're going to the zoo!" Jake shouted, ducking under the covers.

The leopard will lie down with the goat, the calf and the lion and the yearling together;
and a little child will lead them. The cow will feed with the bear, their young will lie down
together, and the lion will eat straw like the ox.... They will neither harm nor destroy on all my
holy mountain, for the earth will be full of the knowledge of the LORD as the waters cover the sea.

ISAIAH 11:6-9

Heaven on Earth

*A*fter church Papa placed his Bible between his seat and Jake's and started the hour's drive to the zoo.

"Papa, will there be animals on the New Earth?"

"Well, it'll be God's original earth remade, just as our new bodies will be our old bodies remade. How similar will the New Earth be to the original earth? We can find the answer to that in what the Bible says about how much our new bodies will be like our old ones. So tell me, Jake—was Christ's resurrection body like his old one?"

"I guess so."

"Sure it was. Adam and Eve ate, drank, walked, and talked. So did Jesus before He died, and then again in His resurrection body. The Bible says our new bodies will be like His, and His was a real human body. Sure, it was more powerful, with some special abilities; it could go through walls, and it'll never die. Our bodies will be glorified, and part of that apparently means they'll be bright. But we'll still have eyes, ears, mouth, nose, arms and legs, hands and feet. And we'll eat and walk and talk. Just as our new bodies will be the same, yet different from our present bodies, the New Earth will be the same, yet different from the present earth."

"So … will there be animals or not?"

Papa laughed. "Okay, my point is, if our new bodies are like our old bodies, we should expect the New Earth to be like the old earth. The question is, how important were animals in God's design for earth? Open my Bible and look at the first chapter, will you? According to Genesis 1:1, what did God create first?"

Jake opened the Bible, but he knew the answer and said it before looking at the page. "The heavens and the earth."

"Right. He shaped the earth and then made plants and trees and living creatures in the water."

"Like whales and dolphins?"

"And fish and turtles. Then what did He make next?"

Jake ran his finger down the page. "Birds?"

"Yep. And on the sixth day of creation He made from earth the land animals, including livestock. I know you love animals, Jake. So do I. But the Bible shows that God loves animals even more. He designed and created them. Tell me what it says about the wild animals."

Jake skimmed down to verse 25. "God made the wild animals and livestock, and He said that it was good."

"And who did God make next?"

Jake read further. "Adam and Eve?"

"Yes. And their job was to take care of the Garden, trees, water, and animals. And to love each other and have children and fill the earth and rule it for God's glory. At the zoo we'll see people who take care of animals. That was a big part of God's job description for Adam and Eve."

"What a great job to have."

"Earth wouldn't be complete without people or animals. God even made animals part of His covenant promise in Genesis 9 after the Flood. So there's every reason to believe they'll be on the New Earth. I think God never changed His opinion about whether a good earth includes animals. I have a big book about all the animals in the Bible. Can you think of some?"

"Camels, donkeys, oxen. Ravens and doves. Sheep and goats. And dogs and bears. And Elijah was taken up to Heaven in a chariot pulled by horses!"

"Very good! In Isaiah 65, where it speaks of the

New Earth, God says animals—a wolf, lamb, and lion among them—will lie down in peace together. Isaiah 11 and 60 both mention animals on a future perfect earth that will last forever. Peter said in Acts 3 that Christ 'must remain in heaven until the time comes for God to restore everything, as he promised long ago through his holy prophets.' The prophets talk about animals living together in peace."

"Do you think Moses will be on the New Earth? I mean, Moses the dog?"

"I wouldn't be surprised. I have great memories of being a boy your age and hanging out with my golden retriever Champ. After looking through my telescope for hours, I'd crawl into my sleeping bag in the backyard and look up at the stars. Champ and I watched lots of meteors together, including some doubles, and he was right beside me when I discovered the Andromeda galaxy. God's touched many people's lives through animals. God can do anything—it'd be simple for Him to recreate a pet in Heaven if He wants to."

"Even Moses?"

"Even Moses … and Champ."

When they got to the zoo, Papa stopped to study a map, but Jake was in a hurry to see everything. He loved the lions, leopards, and Bengal tigers—the elephants, zebras, and laughing hyenas. He watched a meerkat stand on its hind legs. One of the zoo workers brushed a sea lion's teeth. When a giraffe leaned down and stuck out his tongue, Jake put a piece of popcorn on it.

After lunch they found the bird house and stood three feet from a beautiful bald eagle. At the aviary Papa bought a cup of nectar for the lories to drink.

One of the buildings had frogs and lizards. Jake thought the iguanas were cool. Then Papa and Jake watched the otters slide and play and swim on their backs. Papa stopped and prayed, thanking God for creating such funny animals.

Jake and Papa had a blast at the zoo.

Late that afternoon, as they drove home, Papa said, "God's given you a love for animals, Jake. Scripture says we'll have responsibilities when we rule the New Earth. Since ruling includes taking care of animals, I wouldn't be surprised if God gave you that kind of job."

Jake's eyes got big. "Really?"

"Really. You know, lots of kids haven't had the chance to have pets, or maybe they're afraid of animals. Well, the New Earth might be the place where they get to have a pet for the first time. I can picture you right beside Jesus, carrying your soccer ball, walking between a lion and a Bengal tiger, with a dog in the lead. But there's something I want you to read to me from the Bible. Can you find Romans 8?"

Jake whispered names of the New Testament books and then turned to Romans.

"Start at verse 19," Papa said, pointing to the heavily marked paragraph.

"'The creation waits in eager expectation for the sons of God to be revealed. For the creation was subjected to frustration ... the creation itself will be liberated from its bondage to decay and brought into the glorious freedom of the children of God. We know that the whole creation has been groaning as in the pains of childbirth right up to the present time. Not only so, but we ourselves, who have the firstfruits of the Spirit, groan inwardly as we wait eagerly for our adoption as sons, the redemption of our bodies.'"

"Know what that means, Jake?"

"Is it about the resurrection?"

"Exactly! The whole world fell when we humans sinned, and the whole world will rise in our resurrection. Plants and animals suffer and die because of our sin, but when our redemption's complete, all creation will be delivered."

"Including animals?"

"It says the 'whole creation' suffers and longs for deliverance. How could that *not* include animals? It seems to say some animals who were here in this world will be part of the New Earth where they'll no longer suffer. Wouldn't you think some of those animals might be our pets?"

"Like Moses?"

Papa smiled and nodded. "Why not?"

"Will there be dinosaurs on the New Earth?"

"When the curse is lifted, God might recreate some extinct animals. God didn't make a mistake when he first created them. Romans 1:20 says God's invisible qualities, including His power, are clearly seen in His creation. Animals were created for God's glory and to show us what God is like. Wouldn't God's power be shown off in a Tyrannosaur?"

"A T-Rex? On the New Earth?" Now Jake was really excited.

"God created the dinosaurs, and they were all part of a world He called 'very good.' Who knows, maybe on the New Earth you could ride a Brontosaurus or fly on the back of a Pterodactyl."

"Cool!" Jake said. After thinking about this for a minute he asked, "Can we rent a movie, Papa?"

"Which one?"

"*Jurassic Park.*"

Papa laughed. "If you do work with animals on the New Earth, you know who might help you?"

"Who?"

"Your grandmother. She loved animals. I'm sure she still does. I think the two of you would have a blast taking care of God's animals together."

"I know we would." Jake looked at Papa. "Tonight could we sleep out under the stars in sleeping bags? With Moses? And look at the Andromeda galaxy? And watch for meteors?"

"That sounds like fun."

When they got home, they told Moses about the plan. As they were looking up at the stars, Moses kept bringing them a shredded towel to play tug-of-war. Then he'd get out of one sleeping bag and into the other.

Papa and Jake counted a dozen meteors, including a double. They both fell asleep with smiles on their faces. Moses, an old blanket over him, lay between them with his paws straight up, looking at the sky with a snarly grin.

The time came when the beggar died and the angels carried him to Abraham's side.

LUKE 16:22

CHAPTER NINE

The Voyage Home

Papa and Jake sat on the front porch swing. They'd been up early fishing, then picking strawberries. Jake asked Papa for one last batch of waffles. His parents were picking him up in an hour. The two weeks had gone really fast. Moses lay beside Jake, his legs twitching while he dreamed of chasing squirrels.

"In our church," Papa said, "an eight-year-old boy named Brandon died of leukemia just two months after your grandmother. We visited him when he first got sick. I read God's Word to Brandon, and Grammy baked him cookies. I suspect Grammy was part of Brandon's welcoming party in Heaven.

Anyway, the week after Grammy's memorial service, when Brandon heard he was going to die, he cried. He loved Jesus and wanted to be with Him, but he didn't want to leave his family. But his dad had a great idea. He asked Brandon to step through a doorway into another room and then close the door behind him."

"Then what happened?" Jake asked.

"One at a time, the entire family came through the door to join him. Pretty soon everybody was together with him in that other room. His father explained that Brandon would go ahead to Heaven, and the rest would follow. Of course, when we die, we're never left alone. We'll be welcomed by Jesus and our family and friends who've gone before us."

"And angels?"

"The Bible says when Lazarus died, he was taken to Heaven by angels. They were with him all the way. I think your grandmother and Brandon were probably taken to Heaven by angels too. Maybe we'll be carried by the same angels who watch over us here. In fact they're probably here with us right now on this porch."

Jake stuck out his hand. "Maybe my hand's passing through an angel."

Papa chuckled. "I wouldn't be surprised. I think angels have saved my life several times. I want to hear them tell the stories! Think of it. We'll talk and laugh as long as we want. We'll never run out of time. We'll all be part of a great story going on forever. Like C. S. Lewis said, every chapter will be better than the one before."

"I can hardly wait."

"Meanwhile God has a plan for you right here, Jake." Papa opened his Bible. "Second Peter 3:11 says, 'You ought to live holy and godly lives as you look forward to the day of God.' Then it says, 'In keep-

ing with his promise we are looking forward to a new heaven and a new earth, the home of righteousness. So then, dear friends, since you are looking forward to this, make every effort to be found spotless, blameless and at peace with him.' What do you think that means?"

"Maybe … since we're going to live with Jesus forever, we should start living for Him right now?"

"That's a great answer. If we're not looking forward to the New Heavens and New Earth, it's because we just don't get it. Looking forward to Heaven will help us say no to sin and yes to living right. Someday we'll stand before God. If we've put Him first, He'll say, 'Well done, my good and faithful servant; enter into your master's joy.' Can you imagine anything you'd rather hear than that?"

Jake shook his head.

"Me neither." Papa paused to choose his words carefully. "Jake, there's something I want to tell you before your parents get here."

"What, Papa?"

"I'm still strong enough to hike and play tennis and take you to Mexico in December on that mission trip, Lord willing. And my mind's still pretty good.

But maybe in another five or ten years things will change. What I'm trying to say is … your grandma died, and one day I'll die too."

Jake hung his head.

"It's okay. Really. When the time comes, it won't be easy for you. But I want you to hear me say this— your grandfather's not afraid. I know where I'm going and who's waiting for me there. You know where I'm going too, don't you? And as a wise boy recently told me, you haven't lost someone if you know where they've gone!"

Jake smiled.

"I want you to remember something else. If I ever can't get out of bed or can't think straight or if I can't recognize you or your mother anymore, that's just a temporary condition. Don't ever think I'm past my peak. I'll never pass my peak, Jake. The strongest and healthiest I've ever felt is just a hint of what I'll be in my resurrected body on the New Earth. The best is yet to come. Do you understand what I'm saying?"

"Yes," Jake whispered.

"So someday if you hear people say it's too bad Papa can't walk or think straight anymore, you tell them that pretty soon your Papa's going to be a lot stronger and smarter than he ever was!"

"But … I don't want you to die," Jake said. Moses put his head on Jake's lap.

"Dying doesn't excite me either, but what's waiting for me on the other side of death *does*. Jesus. Heaven. Your grandmother. You never knew my parents or my old friends Jerry and Greg, but one day I'll introduce you. I can hardly wait for you to meet them. I may still be around for a long time, but after I'm gone, I want you to remember what we talked about while we picked strawberries, ate waffles, rode in the truck, went to the zoo, and sat in the restaurant."

"And when we climbed to the top of Multnomah Falls?"

"And at our favorite place on the rocks where we star-gazed and saw the double meteors. Whenever you look up at the stars, remember that every clear night your Papa used to step outside and look at those same stars Jesus made. And I'd tell Him I couldn't wait to see His face. When you go home and look at those stars and the Andromeda galaxy, you tell Jesus that same thing. Will you?"

Jake nodded.

"Likely I'll be looking at you from the other side and praying for you too. I want to see you serving King Jesus. You need to study the Bible to know what your King wants you to do. You need to ask for His strength every day and confess your sins so there's nothing between you and God. I pray for you lots, Jake, like I pray for Ty and Matt and Jack. I want to see you all become men of God. I pray that you'll love Jesus with all your hearts. Please pray the same for me. In fact, let's pray for each other right now, okay?"

Papa prayed for Jake; then Jake prayed for Papa. Moses rested his head on his paws like he was praying too.

"Moses is just a pup," Papa said after they finished. "He might live to be fifteen. He could outlive me. I suspect I'll see him again on the New Earth. But meanwhile somebody will need to take care of him. I can't think of anybody I'd rather have keep him than you, Jake. Would you do that for me?"

Jake nodded. Then he hugged Moses, who licked his face.

Papa opened his big red Bible to Revelation 21 and asked Jake to read verses 3 to 5: "'God himself

will be with them and be their God. He will wipe every tear from their eyes. There will be no more death or mourning or crying or pain, for the old order of things has passed away.' He who was seated on the throne said, 'I am making everything new!' Then he said, 'Write this down, for these words are trustworthy and true.'"

"Those are the words of King Jesus, Jake. Count on them. He promises to be with you always. When your time's up here, He'll take you all the way to Heaven. Remember, we were all made for a Person and a place."

Jake smiled and said, "Jesus is the Person. Heaven is the place."

"We'll all be together, and Jesus will be the center of everything, and every day will bring new adventures. Joy will be the air we breathe. And right when we think it can't get any better—it will."

Just then Moses jumped off the swing and ran down the steps, barking and looking toward the far end of the long driveway.

"Here come your mom and dad." Papa put his arm around Jake. "If I get to Heaven before you do, I'll pick out some favorite places to show you, okay?

I imagine your grandma and I will be first in line after Jesus to welcome you. Then one day, after the resurrection, we'll all walk on the New Earth. We'll worship Jesus side by side. Maybe He'll send us places together—or take us there with Him."

"Maybe to the New Andromeda Galaxy," Jake said. "Wouldn't that be great?"

The car was a hundred feet away now.

Papa held up his big red Bible. "I'm going to leave this to you someday, Jake. I hope you'll read it and look at what I underlined and think about me. Remember the good times we had. And look forward to even better times together with Jesus on the New Earth."

Jake's dad and mom got out of the car. Moses jumped all over them, gnawing their shoes. They looked at Papa and Jake on the porch and wondered why the old man and the young boy were crying and laughing at the same time.

The End

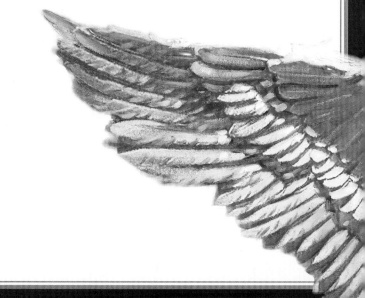

Note from Randy

Many people live as if the present life is all there is. Scripture says, "We are looking forward to a new heavens and new earth, in which righteousness dwells" (2 Peter 3:13).

In *Tell Me About Heaven*, Papa's words to his grandson are grounded in the Bible, the only authoritative word about the afterlife. Their dialogue reflects the kind of conversations I hope to have with my grandsons when they're older.

The best thing we can pass on to our children and grandchildren isn't a big inheritance, but a godly heritage. A huge part of that heritage is helping them love Jesus and live in light of their glorious future with Him and His people. This book is designed to encourage family conversations about Heaven.

It was a joy to work with my friend Ron DiCianni, who proposed this collaboration. Ron and I discussed the paintings in advance, but each time he e-mailed me sketches, they blew me away.

God said of an ancient artist, "I have filled him with the Spirit of God, with skill, ability and knowledge...to make artistic designs...and to engage in all kinds of craftsmanship" (Exodus 31:3-5). I believe God's Spirit worked through Ron to create this magnificent art.

I hope you'll enjoy this story and gaze often and long at these paintings. May they stir your heart and fuel your imagination.

In the New World's never-ending story, as C. S. Lewis put it, every chapter will be better than the one before. To each reader, young or old, who trusts Jesus: I look forward to meeting you there. Meanwhile, never settle for less than what God has in store for you!

Randy Alcorn

www.epm.org

Note from Ron

I can vividly remember the conversations I had with my kids about Heaven over the years. One of these took place while driving to downtown Chicago with one of my sons. I'm not sure which of us was more uncomfortable with the topic. I can tell you this, however, that he was more honest than I expected, and I was more uncomfortable than he expected. I knew this was no ordinary conversation where I could give vague answers; this was a pivotal moment that would "make or break" his concept of Heaven forever. It was daunting. If I could go back in time and do that conversation over, I'd bring this book with me.

I don't think much has changed during the years since that time. Parents still have the challenging task of teaching their children about eternity, and kids still want to know. Some kids are just too scared to ask and would rather not think about it, until they have to. But God didn't mean for them, or us, to be ignorant of what lies ahead. Vague descriptions and hopeful phrases don't cut it either. You know what I am talking about—phrases like: "It's going to be so great," "You just can't imagine...," or "It's way better than anything we know now." We all need and want more than that. And God gave it to us in the Bible, but somewhere, somehow, we developed bad theology concerning Heaven. Floating on clouds as a disembodied spirit, playing harps, and one long church service is pretty much the extent of what we think about Heaven, and all of that is wrong!

What would your child say if you said that his or her best friend went to live permanently at the North Pole with Santa Claus. (I think the answer would be something close to "Awesome!" accompanied by a bit of envy.) Or say that his or her best friend's father got a job at Disney World, and the family is going to live in the actual park from now on! (Chances are, your child might ask if you could get a job like that!)

Now tell your child that his or her best friend went to be with Jesus in Heaven. (If I am correct, tears would flow, and he or she might experience a lot of fear.) How sad. The greatest of all three options gets the worst reaction, because we gave the wrong impression of the life hereafter. Inexcusable! Now you can change your children's opinion of Heaven forever with Randy's amazing book. They will see that the best is yet to come.

www.tapestryproductions.com